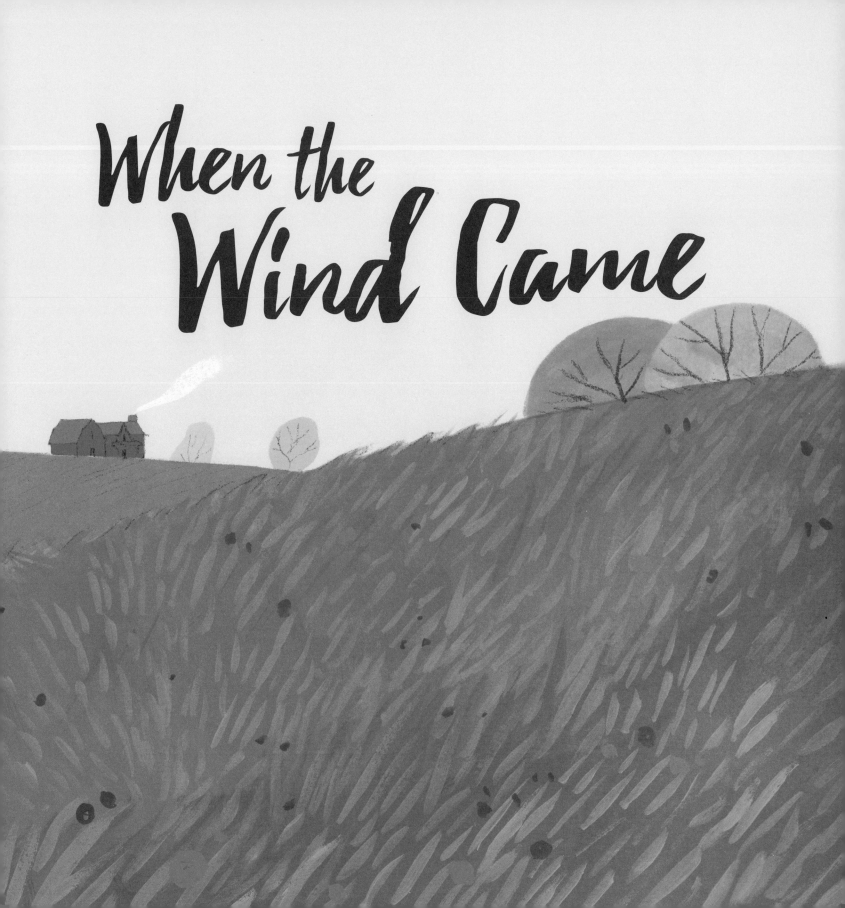

When the Wind Came

For everyone, everywhere, who stands with courage and even laughter in the face of the devouring winds of change — J.C. for J.A.

For my family — D.L.

Published in Canada and the U.S. by Kids Can Press Ltd.
25 Dockside Drive, Toronto, ON M5A 0B5

Kids Can Press is a Corus Entertainment Inc. company
www.kidscanpress.com

The artwork in this book was rendered in pencil and paint.
The text is set in Minion Pro.

Edited by Yasemin Uçar
Designed by Barb Kelly

Printed and bound in Buji, Shenzhen, China,
in 10/2021 by WKT Company

CM 22 0 9 8 7 6 5 4 3 2 1

FSC
www.fsc.org
MIX
Paper from
responsible sources
FSC® C010256

Library and Archives Canada Cataloguing in Publication

Title: When the wind came / written by Jan Andrews ; illustrated by Dorothy Leung.
Names: Andrews, Jan, author. | Leung, Dorothy, illustrator.
Identifiers: Canadiana 20210214805 | ISBN 9781525303395 (hardcover)
Classification: LCC PS8551.N37 W545 2022 | DDC jC813/.54 — dc23

Kids Can Press gratefully acknowledges that the land on which our office is located is the traditional territory of many nations, including the Mississaugas of the Credit, the Anishnabeg, the Chippewa, the Haudenosaunee and the Wendat peoples, and is now home to many diverse First Nations, Inuit and Métis peoples.

We thank the Government of Ontario, through Ontario Creates; the Ontario Arts Council; the Canada Council for the Arts; and the Government of Canada for supporting our publishing activity.

When the Wind Came

Written by Jan Andrews

Illustrated by Dorothy Leung

Kids Can Press

I remember my father
shouting at the cattle.

I remember my mother
tearing at the weeds.

I remember my baby brother
whimpering,
whimpering,
whimpering.

Every day,
every day,
every day.

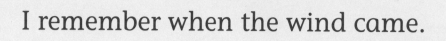

I remember when the wind came.

I remember it blowing
harder
and harder
and harder.

I remember my mother
grabbing up my baby brother.

I remember her running
with him in her arms.

I remember my father opening
the door to the root cellar.

I remember sitting in the darkness.

I remember the silence over us.
I wanted to say something.
I couldn't. I didn't know how.

Our home was gone
when we came out.

Somehow out of the
ruin, my mother made
us something to eat.

It was my job
to do the dishes.

I found soap in the rubble.
I found water and a bowl.

I don't know why I did it.
I wasn't even thinking.
Maybe I was crying.
Maybe tears were running down my cheeks.

Maybe the only thing I felt like was making a circle with my thumb and first finger and …

blowing a bubble.

One, two

and then another.

My baby brother was giggling.
He was reaching toward the
bubbles that I'd made.

My father let out a laugh.
My mother laughed with him.

Those laughs didn't change anything.
They made no difference.

Those laughs changed
everything.

They made all the
difference in the world.